LET'S-READ-AND-FIND-OUT SCIENCE®

STAGE 1

IS THERE LIFE IN OUTER SPACE?

by Franklyn M. Branley

illustrated by Edward Miller

HARPERCOLLINS*PUBLISHERS*

For Claire Elizabeth Pellegrini—Welcome

—F.B.

To my sister Diane

—E.M.

Special thanks to Jurrie van der Woude
at the National Aeronautics and Space Administration for his expert advice.

The art in this book was computer generated using Adobe Illustrator.

Photo credits: Pages 13, 14, 16, 17, 19, 28, and 29 are from the National Aeronautics and Space Administration.

HarperCollins®, ☂®, and Let's Read-and-Find-Out Science® are trademarks of HarperCollins Publishers Inc.

The *Let's-Read-and-Find-Out Science* book series was originated by Dr. Franklyn M. Branley, Astronomer Emeritus and former Chairman of the American Museum—Hayden Planetarium, and was formerly co-edited by him and Dr. Roma Gans, Professor Emeritus of Childhood Education, Teachers College, Columbia University. Text and illustrations for each of the books in the series are checked for accuracy by an expert in the relevant field. For more information about Let's-Read-and-Find-Out Science books, write to HarperCollins Children's Books, 195 Broadway, New York, NY 10007.

IS THERE LIFE IN OUTER SPACE?

Library of Congress Cataloging-in-Publication Data Branley, Franklyn Mansfield, 1915– Is there life in outer space? / by Franklyn M. Branley;
illustrated by Edward Miller.   p.   cm. — (Let's-read-and-find-out science. Stage 1)   Previously published: New York, Crowell, c1984.
Summary: Discusses some of the ideas and misconceptions about life in outer space and speculates on the existence of such life
in light of recent space explorations.   ISBN 0-06-028146-4. — ISBN 0-06-445192-5 (pbk.) — ISBN 0-06-028145-6 (lib. bdg.)
1. Life on other planets—Juvenile literature. [1. Life on other planets. 2. Outer space—Exploration.]
I. Miller, Edward, 1964– ill. II. Title. III. Series. QB54.B694 1999
99-10904   576.8'39—dc21   CIP   AC

Typography by Edward Miller
16 17 18 SCP 20 19 18
❖
Newly illustrated edition

IS THERE LIFE IN OUTER SPACE?

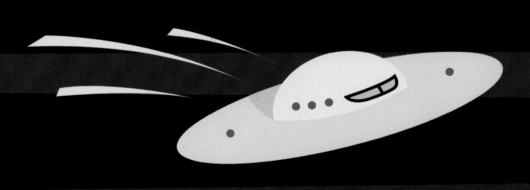

Bears and birds, bugs and toads, trees, flowers,
people, and lots of other things live on planet Earth.
Do they live anywhere else? Do plants and animals live on
the moon? Do they live on Mars or Jupiter or any other planet?
Or do they live far away out among the stars?
For a long time people have wondered about that.
Maybe you have, too.

More than a hundred years ago a newspaper said plants and animals lived on the moon. An astronomer could see them through a big, new telescope.

There were trees on the moon, the newspaper said. Big melons grew on them. Animals that looked like small buffaloes grazed beneath the trees. Animals that looked like bears walked around on their hind legs.

There were people, too. They had hair all over their bodies, and they had wings. The moon people were friendly, the story said. Some of them sat near a pond feeding melons to one another.

The story wasn't true. But for a long time, people believed in these moon creatures.

9

People also believed a radio story that said Martians had landed on Earth. The Martians had big heads and small bodies. They came in spaceships. They were not friendly. Once they landed, they spread out and attacked people in towns and villages.

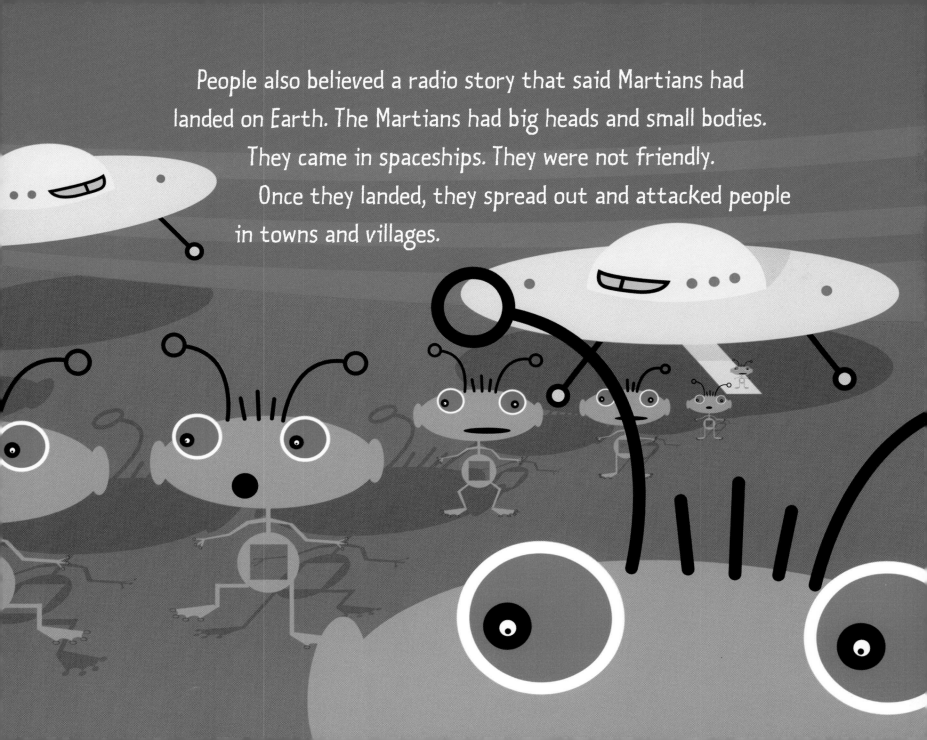

By the 1960's, only a few people still believed there were Martians or moon people. In 1969, everyone knew for sure that there was no life of any kind on the moon. That was the year Neil Armstrong and Edwin Aldrin walked on the moon.

13

After them, other
astronauts went to the moon. No matter
where they looked, the astronauts found nothing
alive. They found no sign that plants or animals
had ever lived there. The moon is a
dead world, and it always has been.
But, people said, that does not mean there is no
other life in our whole solar system. Mars is like Earth in many ways.
Maybe there are plants there. Maybe there are animals, too—
although no one expected they would look
like the Martians with big heads.

Pictures of Mars show places
where water once flowed. Where there
is water, there may also be plants and animals.
Did plants and animals once live on Mars?
Could they be living there still?
Space probes were sent to Mars to find out.
More pictures were taken. The soil of Mars was
tested. No plants or animals of any kind were
seen in the pictures. No signs of life
were found in the soil.

ON MARS:

TERRAIN

FROST

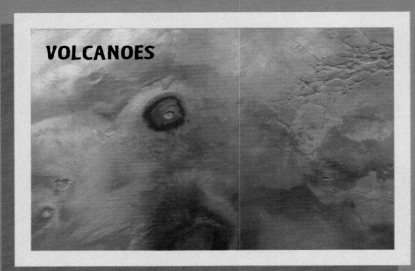

VOLCANOES

CRATERS

But what about the other planets? Perhaps there is life on Venus. Or maybe Mercury has plants and animals.

A probe was sent to Mercury to get a closer look. This is a picture it took.

Mercury doesn't look like a place where plants or animals could live. It looks like the dead world of the moon. Also, Mercury gets very hot, much too hot for anything to live there.

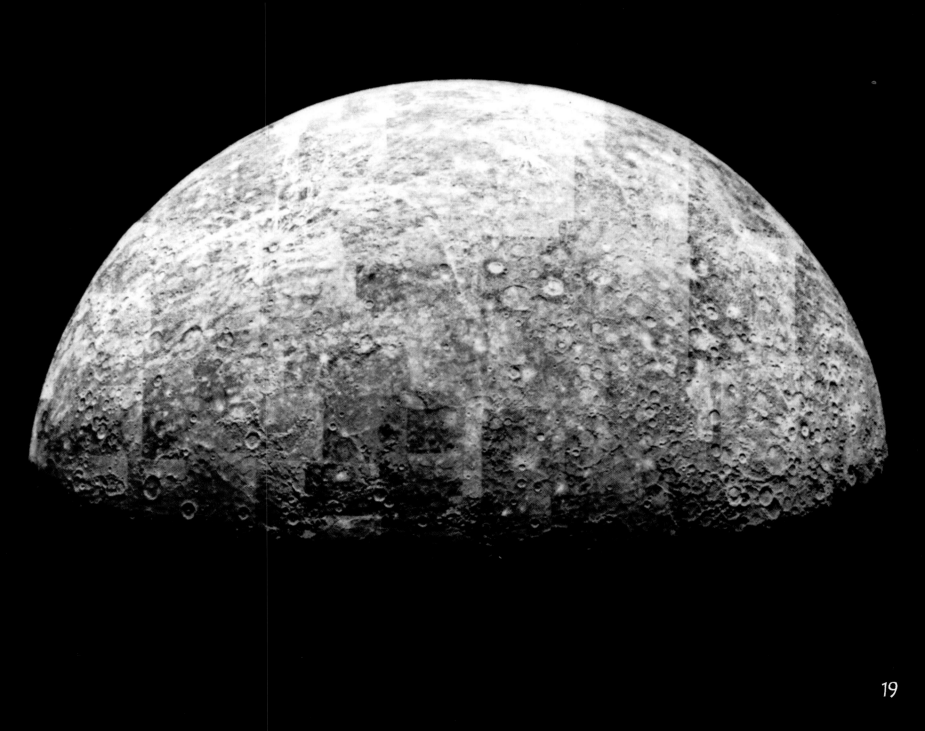

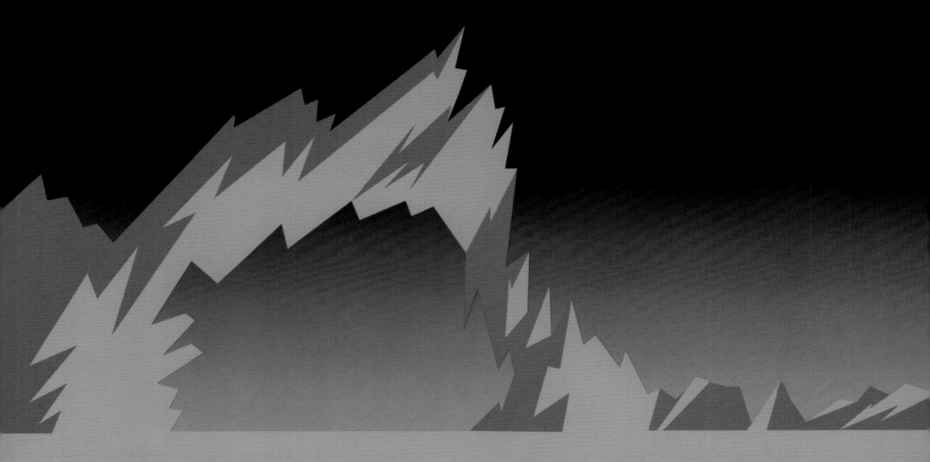

Probes were landed on Venus, too. It is so hot on Venus that parts of some probes melted when they landed. Also, poison gases are all around the planet. No signs of life have ever been found on Venus.

No one expects there could be life on any of the other planets in our solar system.

SUN

Mercury

Venus

Earth

Mars

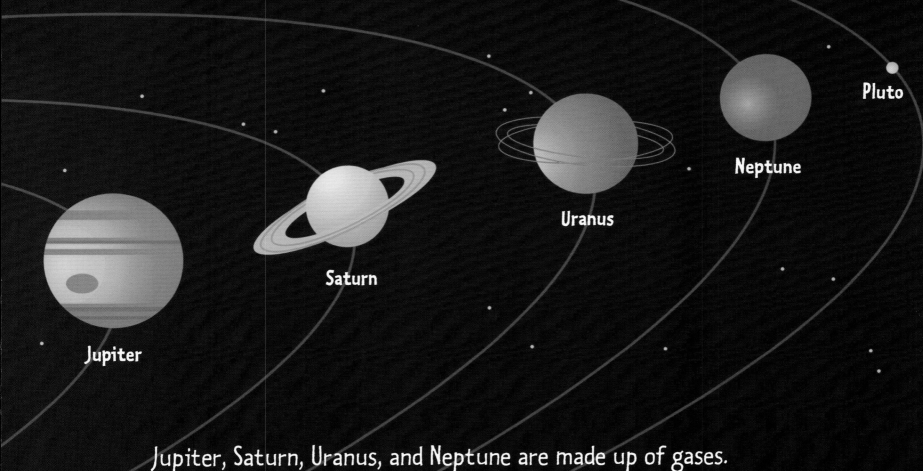

Jupiter, Saturn, Uranus, and Neptune are made up of gases. All of these planets are also very cold, much colder than any place on Earth. And so is tiny Pluto.

In our solar system, Earth seems to be the only planet where we know for sure there is life.

But there are billions of stars
beyond our solar system.

There are planets going around some of
these stars, just as Earth goes around the sun.

Plants and animals may live on some of them.
We don't know for sure because we can't see the
planets very well.

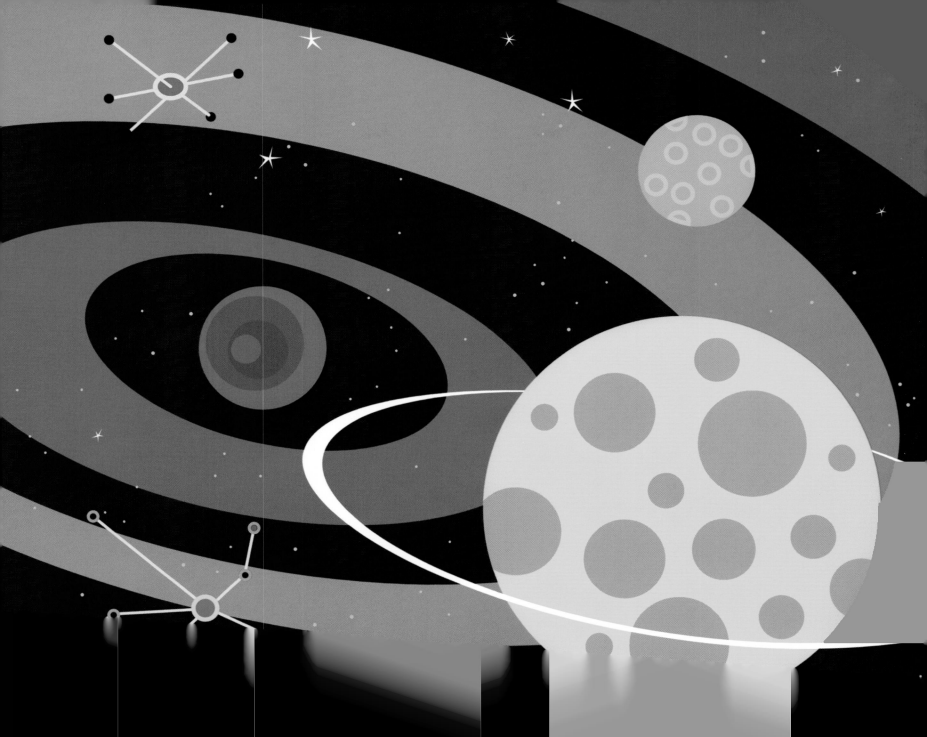

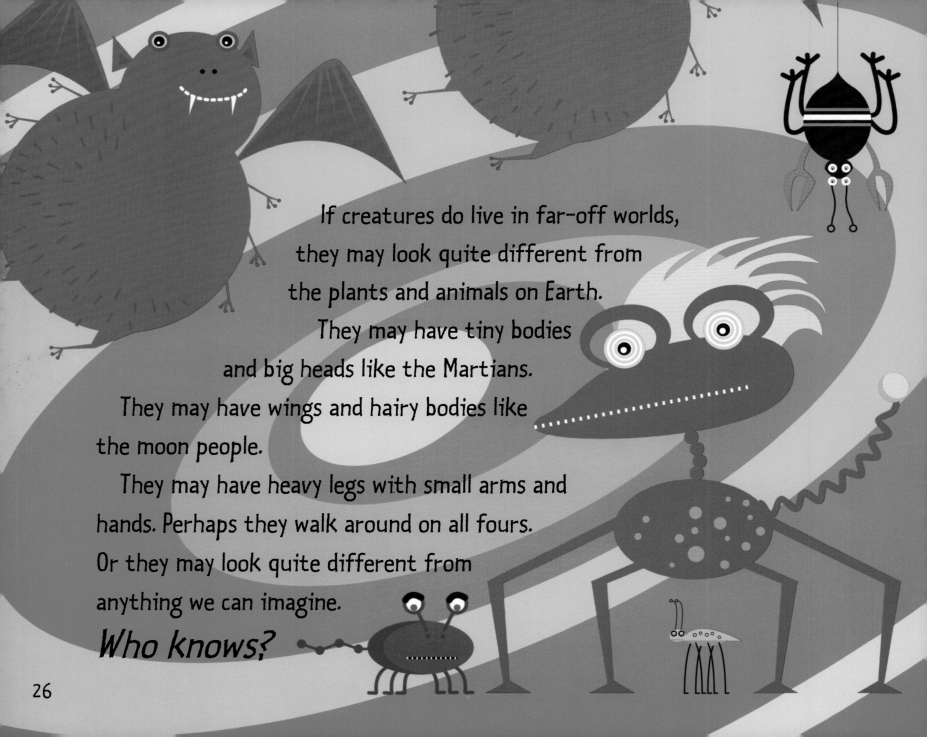

If creatures do live in far-off worlds,
they may look quite different from
the plants and animals on Earth.
They may have tiny bodies
and big heads like the Martians.
They may have wings and hairy bodies like
the moon people.
They may have heavy legs with small arms and
hands. Perhaps they walk around on all fours.
Or they may look quite different from
anything we can imagine.
Who knows?

27

Some people think it's silly to believe there are planets beyond our solar system. But there are. Many have been discovered. People also say it's silly to believe there is life on them. But I don't think so.

It seems that somewhere out among the billions of stars, there must be plants and animals living on other worlds. There may be creatures that know as much as we do. Some may be a lot smarter.

One day we may be able to talk with them.

Many years from now we may even travel to those far-off planets and land on them. That's what I think.

What do you think?

FIND OUT MORE ABOUT LIFE IN OUTER SPACE

- Draw a picture of a space suit that you would wear to look for life on planets in other galaxies. Remember that you will not be on Earth, where you have everything you need to stay alive. The suit will need to give you air, food, water, and keep your body from getting too hot or too cold.

- If creatures were found on another planet, how would you communicate with them? What would you tell them about yourself and about life on Earth? Would your life be the same or different?

- If you discovered a new planet, what might it be like? Imagine and draw a picture of it. What do the living things look like? Are there birds, bees, and bugs? How do the creatures move and eat?

- Check out what's happening at your local planetarium. You may find an exhibit or program about the search for life on other planets.